Ballet Bullies

BY JAKE MADDOX

illustrated by Tuesday Mourning

text by Emma Carlson Berne

STONE ARCH BOOKS
www.stonearchbooks.com

Impact Books are published by Stone Arch Books
151 Good Counsel Drive, P.O. Box 669
Mankato, Minnesota 56002
www.stonearchbooks.com

Library of Congress Cataloging-in-Publication Data
Maddox, Jake.
 Ballet bullies / by Jake Maddox ; text by Emma Carlson Berne ; illustrated
by Tuesday Mourning.
    p. cm. — (Impact books. A Jake Maddox sports story)
  ISBN 978-1-4342-1604-5
 [1. Ballet dancing—Fiction.] I. Berne, Emma Carlson. II. Mourning,
Tuesday, ill. III. Title.
  PZ7.M25643Bal 2010
  [Fic]—dc22
                                            2009004080

Summary:
Marissa has always loved dancing. But lately, she feels clumsy and awkward
when she dances, and she feels bigger and taller than the other girls. She
doesn't even bother trying out for the Rose Fairy ballet. But someone else
thinks Marissa has what it takes to play the Rose Fairy!

Creative Director: Heather Kindseth
Graphic Designer: Emily Harris

Photo Credit: Capstone Press/Karon Dubke, cover (background)

Printed in the United States of America

TABLE OF CONTENTS

Chapter 1

DANCING DILEMMA

The ballerinas stuffed their dance bags inside their lockers and slammed the gray metal doors. All the dancers at Madame Stone's ballet studio were ready for their after-school practice — except for Marissa.

As the other girls left the changing room, laughing and talking to each other, Marissa stood at her locker. She held her practice outfit in her hands.

Everyone had to wear the same thing: a black leotard, pink tights, and pink ballet slippers. Warm-ups were about to start in the big exercise room next door, but Marissa was still wearing the comfortable sweatpants and T-shirt she had worn to school that day.

A girl with a freckled face looked around the door. "Hey there," Marissa's best friend, Rachel, said. "Warm-ups are starting. You know Madame hates it when we're late."

Marissa looked up. "I know, Rachel. I just can't," she said.

Rachel walked into the room. She sat down on the bench next to Marissa. "You can't what?" she asked gently.

"I can't put on the practice outfit," Marissa explained. She stared down at the black leotard and pink tights.

"Why not?" Rachel asked. "We all wear that outfit every day. You've been dancing here forever. What's the matter?"

Marissa sighed. "I just feel weird putting on the leotard and dancing in front of everyone. I feel like the other girls are staring at me," she admitted.

Rachel put her arm around her friend's shoulders and gave her a hug. She knew that Marissa felt self-conscious about her body.

Over the last year, Marissa had grown a lot taller and bigger than the other girls in the ballet studio. She was almost as tall as Madame Stone, their dance teacher.

"Don't worry about it so much," Rachel told Marissa. "You love dancing. Just think about the music and the steps."

Marissa stood up. She quickly stuffed the leotard and tights back into her locker. Then she shut the metal door. "Okay, I'm ready," she said.

"But you didn't change," Rachel said.

Marissa started walking toward the exercise room. "I'll just dance in my sweatpants and T-shirt," she said. "I told you, I don't want to put on the leotard."

"But Madame Stone has rules about what we wear!" Rachel protested, following her friend.

"Maybe she won't care," Marissa said. She pushed open the door to the practice room.

"She'll care," Rachel said quietly.

Chapter 2

PRACTICE PROBLEMS

Marissa hurried into the big exercise room. The walls were covered with mirrors and lined with ballet barres. Andy, the piano player, was playing some lively music.

The other girls were already warming up. They stood in front of the mirrors, holding on to the barres.

Madame Stone called out, "And *plie* one, and *plie* two."

Marissa hurried to an empty spot in the corner. She hoped Madame wouldn't notice her sweatpants right away.

Marissa put one hand lightly on the barre and began her *plies*. She carefully held her feet in first position.

Suddenly, she realized that Madame Stone had stopped counting and was staring at her. All of the other girls stopped their exercises and turned around to look.

"Marissa," Madame Stone said, "where is your leotard and tights?"

Marissa could feel her cheeks turning red. She stared at the floor.

Madame Stone gave her a long look. "Oh well," Madame said. "If you forgot your leotard, it doesn't really matter for this one class."

She turned back to the rest of the students. "Girls! Pay attention! Ready and go," Madame instructed.

Marissa slid one leg out to the side and back again, being careful to point her toe each time. She stared at herself in the mirror as she practiced. Marissa could see that she was at least six inches taller than the other girls around her. She was also heavier. Everyone else looked like butterflies, but she felt like an elephant.

"Marissa," Madame Stone called. "We are ready to start our practice routines. Would you please show us the first steps of routine A?"

After the warm-ups at the barre, the dancers always moved out into the center of the big, open floor. They practiced more complicated jumps, leaps, and turns.

Usually, this was Marissa's favorite part of the class. Madame Stone often asked her to demonstrate certain moves. Marissa had always loved it. But ever since she started growing so much, Marissa had been dreading dancing in front of everyone. She felt like a giant, thundering creature, not a graceful ballerina.

But she knew she had no choice. Madame Stone was waiting for her. So was the rest of the class.

She slowly walked to the front of the room as Andy began the music. As she lifted her right leg, Marissa saw Kelly and Clarice. They were whispering to each other and giggling.

They're talking about how I look up here, Marissa thought as she began to dance. She stumbled and fell to her knees.

Madame Stone signaled to Andy to stop playing. "Marissa, are you all right?" she asked.

Marissa quickly got to her feet. "I'm fine, Madame," she said. Rachel gave her an encouraging smile. Kelly and Clarice were still laughing.

Madame started the music again. This time, Marissa couldn't find the rhythm. She fumbled through the arabesques and leaps as fast as she could. All she wanted to do was finish the demonstration.

When Marissa was done, Madame was quiet. Marissa could tell she knew something was wrong.

Finally, Madame said, "Thank you, Marissa. Let's have everyone on their feet to try this routine."

For the rest of class, Marissa tried to forget about Kelly and Clarice.

At the end of class, Madame Stone clapped her hands. "Girls, give me your attention, please," she said. "Our recital is coming up soon. This is the time when we show our family and friends the progress we have made in ballet."

Marissa looked around. All of the dancers started whispering with excitement.

"The piece we are going to perform this year is called *The Rose Fairy*," Madame Stone went on. "The dance tells the story of a Rose Fairy. She has lost her other flower friends and is looking for them. If you want to dance in the recital, you'll have to try out for the part. The auditions will be next week. That's it. See you girls tomorrow."

Everyone got up and started heading toward the locker room. Clarice and Kelly brushed by Marissa. As they passed, Marissa saw Clarice glance at her and then whisper to Kelly. They both burst into laughter. Marissa felt her face heat up.

"Marissa," said Madame Stone. "Can I see you for a moment?"

Chapter 3

MARISSA AND THE ROSE FAIRY

Madame Stone's office was small and messy. There were papers everywhere. Pictures of famous ballerinas covered the walls.

"Sit down, Marissa," Madame said. Marissa perched on a chair in front of Madame's big wooden desk.

Madame folded her hands and leaned forward. "Why aren't you wearing your practice leotard?" she asked gently.

Marissa felt her face get hot. She looked down at the ground.

"I expect all the students to be properly dressed for dancing," Madame Stone went on. "You know the rules."

Marissa didn't know what to say. How could she tell Madame that she felt weird about how her body looked in the leotard? It was way too embarrassing.

Madame Stone waited for a minute. When Marissa didn't say anything, Madame said, "I could tell that something was upsetting you today. Your dancing wasn't like it usually is."

"I'm sorry, Madame," Marissa said softly.

Her teacher nodded. "It's okay, Marissa." She paused for a moment.

Then she said, "I don't mind if you want to wear a T-shirt and sweatpants to practice for a while. But if you want to dance in the recital, you'll have to wear a costume, just like everyone else."

Marissa nodded, but her heart was sinking right into her ballet slippers. Of course she wanted to dance in the recital. But she'd seen the costumes. They were all leotards.

Rachel was waiting in the locker room. "I'm so excited about the recital!" she squealed. Marissa took her dance bag out of her locker. Then she and Rachel headed outside.

"Yeah, me too, I guess," Marissa said quietly. She stared at the sidewalk as she trudged along.

"You don't sound very excited," Rachel said.

"I think maybe I'll skip the recital this year. It's no big deal," Marissa said. She tried to sound as if she really didn't care.

"What?" Rachel asked. She stared at her friend. "What are you talking about? You're the best dancer in the studio. How can you skip the recital?"

"You saw how badly I danced today," Marissa said. "Clarice and Kelly were whispering, and I felt so weird up there. I even messed up that easy little dance I was demonstrating."

"Who cares about Clarice and Kelly?" Rachel said. "You're a way better dancer than either of them. That's why Madame Stone always asks you to demonstrate. They're probably just jealous."

"Maybe," Marissa said. "Let's just drop it, okay?"

Rachel was quiet for a few minutes. Suddenly, she said, "I've got it! You should try out for the Rose Fairy part!"

"Ha!" Marissa said. "Very funny. There's no way Madame would ever give me the lead part in the recital. Not after the way I danced today."

"That was just a demonstration in class!" Rachel exclaimed. "What matters is how you do in the auditions."

Marissa shook her head. "I've seen the Rose Fairy costume," she said. "It's a red leotard, with red tights and a pink tutu. I can't wear that. I feel like an elephant in my practice leotard. The costume would be even worse."

"Whatever," Rachel said, waving her hand. "You can dance that part better than anyone else in the studio, including Clarice and Kelly. And me, for that matter."

"It'll never work, Rachel," Marissa said. "Just forget it."

Chapter 4

AUDITION WORRIES

Over the next few days, Marissa couldn't stop thinking about the recital auditions. Even in math class, she drew pictures of ballerinas in her notebook when she should have been paying attention to algebra.

Maybe I should try out for the Rose Fairy part, Marissa thought. *Maybe I'd even get it.* But then what would she do about the costume? How would she dance in front of everyone?

At lunch each day, all Rachel could talk about was the audition and the recital. Rachel had decided to try out for the part of the Daisy Maiden, one of the Rose Fairy's lost friends.

Every day, she asked Marissa if she had decided to try out for the Rose Fairy part. Every day, Marissa shook her head.

The morning of auditions, Marissa woke up feeling good. She felt strong and bold, just like the clear day outside. That was a good sign.

She decided that she would try out for the Rose Fairy part. Rachel was right. Marissa could dance the part. She might as well try out.

On the way to school, Marissa told Rachel her decision. Rachel shrieked.

She did a leap right in the middle of the sidewalk. "Now we can be in the recital together!" Rachel said, hugging Marissa.

"If I get the part," Marissa said. "I still have to try out."

"You'll get the part," Rachel told her. "I just know it."

* * *

After school, Marissa went straight to the ballet studio. She wanted to warm up a little before the audition started.

In the empty locker room, she stuffed her bag into her locker. Then she pulled on her T-shirt and sweatpants. She was lacing up her slippers when the door opened.

Marissa looked up. Clarice and Kelly were walking in.

Marissa quickly looked down again. Instead of going to their own lockers, Clarice and Kelly stopped right next to Marissa.

Kelly put her hands on her hips. "So, Marissa, are you going to audition in your sweatpants?" she asked nastily. Clarice giggled.

"So what if I am?" Marissa mumbled.

"You should wear a leotard like everyone else," Kelly said.

"Madame said I could wear this to practice in," Marissa replied. She forced herself to look Kelly in the eye. "Anyway, it's none of your business."

"Maybe you think you're too good to wear the same thing as the rest of us," Clarice chimed in.

"Or maybe Marissa just outgrew her leotard. Now she can't find one in a big enough size!" Kelly said. She and Clarice burst out laughing and walked away.

Marissa couldn't keep the tears from piling up in her eyes.

That's it, she thought. *There's no way I can audition now.*

If those two were laughing at her, how many other people would be too? Why should she put herself through the humiliation of an audition?

There's no way Madame Stone would give the part to me, she thought sadly.

Chapter 5

DANCE YOUR HEART OUT

Marissa walked into the practice room. She planned to find Madame. She'd tell her she wouldn't be trying out for the recital this year. But Madame was nowhere to be seen.

Andy was sitting at the piano, playing for a few girls who were warming up. As Marissa stood in the corner, she noticed what Andy was playing. It was "The Flower Theme."

The Rose Fairy danced to the song at the end of the ballet. Marissa had heard "The Flower Theme" before. It sounded different when Andy played it. It seemed more alive, somehow.

Marissa felt the music flooding through her body. It reached the tips of her toes. Her feet tingled. She felt light but strong, like a wire stretched tight. Andy pounded out the tune.

Suddenly, Marissa couldn't help herself. She lifted her arms in the air and twirled around. Then she leapt across the floor in a series of jumps.

Marissa could tell that the other dancers had stopped their warm-ups and were watching her, but she didn't care. All she cared about was that she was dancing the way she used to.

It felt good. Andy played the last few notes. Marissa swept into an arabesque. She held the pose for a few seconds and then relaxed.

The clapping startled her. She looked around. The rest of the class had gathered by the door leading to the locker room. Marissa could see Rachel grinning and clapping.

Kelly and Clarice were standing to one side of the group, their arms folded. They were the only girls who weren't clapping or smiling.

Marissa suddenly remembered what had happened in the locker room. She could feel herself deflate, as if she were a balloon that had been popped. She was back in reality now. The world of music she'd lived in for a few minutes while she danced was gone.

The other girls started trickling into the practice room to begin warming up for the auditions.

Marissa looked around for Madame Stone. She spotted her standing near the piano, talking quietly with Andy.

Marissa walked over. "Madame Stone," she said, "I just wanted to tell you that I won't be trying out for the recital this year."

The words were hard to say. Marissa felt like she had to drag them out of herself.

Madame raised her eyebrows. She nodded slowly. "Are you sure, Marissa?" she asked.

Marissa told herself not to cry. "Yeah," she whispered, staring down at her ballet slippers.

She turned and ran to the locker room. As she pulled her dance bag from her locker, she could hear Madame giving the instructions for the auditions.

Marissa shut her locker door and left the building. It was weird walking home without Rachel. Slowly, she started trudging down the sidewalk toward home.

Chapter 6

SURPRISE!

The next afternoon, Marissa didn't bother going to the ballet studio for class.

They'll just be practicing for the recital, she thought. *There's no point in going to class. I'll just go home.*

She left school before Rachel could catch up with her. She didn't even want to talk to her best friend. She knew it might hurt Rachel's feelings, but she just wanted to get home.

At home, Marissa went straight to her room and closed the door. She lay on her bed and mashed her face into her pillow. She tried not to think of everyone else at ballet practice, dancing and having a good time without her.

The phone next to her bed rang. Marissa picked it up. It was Rachel.

"Marissa!" Rachel almost screamed. "You have to get to the studio right now!"

Marissa sat up. "Why?" she asked. "What's going on?"

"I can't say anything more," Rachel said. "Just get down here right away." She hung up.

Marissa leapt off her bed and grabbed her dance bag. She pounded down the stairs and ran out the front door.

She jogged all the way to the studio. *Why is Rachel so excited?* she wondered. *Why do I have to get there right away?*

After five minutes, Marissa was at the studio. She peeked into the practice room. All of the dancers were gathered around a sheet of paper tacked to the bulletin board at one end of the room.

Rachel pushed her way through the group. She grabbed Marissa by the hand and dragged her over to the bulletin board.

"Look at this!" Rachel said. She pointed at the paper. Marissa leaned closer and peered at it. It was a list of the dancers and their parts for the recital.

The first name on the list was Marissa's. Next to it was written "Rose Fairy."

Chapter 7

MADAME INSISTS

Marissa felt her jaw drop. How could she have gotten the part? She hadn't auditioned.

She could hardly think about it because Rachel was pulling her into a crazy dance in the middle of the floor.

"This is incredible!" Rachel said after she finally stopped twirling Marissa around. "I knew you'd get the part."

"I think it's a mistake," Marissa said. "I didn't try out! How could I get the lead role without even auditioning? I told Madame I wasn't going to be in the recital."

"Who cares?" Rachel asked. "You've got the lead! Aren't you happy?"

"Yes," Marissa admitted. "But I'd better go talk to Madame."

"She's in her office," Rachel said. "She said we'd take the day off from practice. Rehearsals for the recital start tomorrow."

"Thanks," Marissa said. "Will you wait for me?"

"Of course," Rachel said, smiling.

Marissa knocked on Madame's office door. Her teacher looked up. "Hi, Marissa," she said. "I was expecting you."

Marissa sat down.

"I know what you want to talk about," Madame Stone said. "You got the part of the Rose Fairy because you are the dancer who deserves it most. I saw your warm-up dance before the audition. You captured the spirit of the role. You danced every step beautifully."

"But I was just playing around a little," Marissa protested. "It wasn't a real audition. I just heard Andy playing, and I couldn't help dancing."

"That's exactly what I mean," Madame said. "The music inspired you to dance. That is one of the qualities of a great dancer. I think you could be a great dancer. But you can't let your lack of confidence stop you."

"But Madame, I wasn't even going to be in the recital at all," Marissa said.

Madame frowned. "I want you in that part," she said. "I expect you to be here at every rehearsal, dancing your very best. That is all." She turned back to the papers on her desk.

"Okay," Marissa whispered. She got up and left the room.

Rachel was waiting for her outside the building. "What did she say?" Rachel asked. The two turned and started walking down the sidewalk.

"She said that I got the part because I deserved it, and I have to dance the role," Marissa said. "This is going to be hard. I mean, it's not that I can't do the steps. I know I can."

"So what's the problem?" Rachel asked.

Marissa sighed. "It's just that when I get up there in front of everyone, I feel so big and awkward," she said. "I feel like everyone's wondering what I'm doing onstage. And the costume is that red leotard. Everyone will laugh when they see me in it!"

"You have to stop worrying," Rachel said. "No one's laughing at you."

"Clarice and Kelly are," Marissa replied.

Rachel rolled her eyes. "Those girls make fun of everyone," she said. "Are you really going to let two immature girls ruin your chances at dancing the lead in the biggest recital of the year?"

"No, I guess not," Marissa said slowly. She paused.

Then she said, "I don't know how I'm going to do it. Maybe Madame will let me dance in a closet or something."

"Don't count on it," Rachel said. "Besides, we've got a lot of practicing to do. The recital's only a week away!"

Chapter 8

MARISSA'S MESS

At rehearsals that week, no one said anything more to Marissa about the Rose Fairy part, including Madame.

Marissa sometimes saw Clarice and Kelly staring while she practiced. She tried to ignore them.

While she danced, Marissa tried to put everything out of her mind except the music and the steps.

Sometimes, she even danced with her eyes closed. That way, she could really pretend she was the Rose Fairy.

But even with all her hard work, something still wasn't right. She still couldn't feel the music in her body the way she had the day of auditions. She was distracted by feeling like she was much bigger and taller than everyone else around her.

During practice one day, Madame Stone told Andy to stop the music.

"No, no, no, Marissa!" Madame called across the stage. "You're just dancing the steps. Anyone can do that. I want you to be inspired by the character. I want you to become the Rose Fairy."

"Okay, Madame," Marissa said.

She saw Clarice whisper something to Kelly. Marissa's face turned hot. She danced worse than ever after that, even stumbling on an easy plie.

* * *

On Friday, Marissa walked to school with Rachel. "I can't believe the recital is today," Rachel said. "I couldn't go to sleep last night until midnight. I was so nervous. Are you scared?"

"I'm terrified," Marissa confessed. "My whole family is coming. A ton of kids from school will be there. And I still haven't tried on the Rose Fairy costume!" She shook her head and went on, "Plus, I've been dancing horribly this week. You saw how Madame yelled at me the other day. This whole thing is going to be a disaster."

"You've got to stop beating yourself up," Rachel said. "Maybe you'll feel different once you get onstage tonight."

"Yeah. I'll probably feel worse!" Marissa said.

Marissa did her class work in a fog that day. She barely heard anything her teachers said.

After school, she went straight home. She wanted to rest and eat dinner before the recital.

At dinner, Marissa could barely choke down her chicken and baked potato. She felt sick every time she thought about the recital. She asked to be excused as soon as she could.

"Of course, honey," her dad said. "We'll see you at the studio soon."

The dancers had to be at the studio early to get their costumes on and to hear last-minute instructions from Madame. Marissa's family would come later.

Marissa hurried to the studio alone. The building was all lit up, and warm yellow squares of light from the windows lay on the sidewalk.

Inside, the place was full of dancers. Parents were standing around, and eager grandparents were already snapping pictures.

Marissa pushed her way through the crowd to the locker room. Madame was handing out the costumes.

"Hi, Marissa," Madame said. "Here's the Rose Fairy costume." She handed Marissa the red leotard, red tights, and pink tutu.

Marissa put the costume down on the bench in front of her locker. All around her, girls were pulling on their own costumes. Marissa felt a soft hand on her shoulder. She looked up.

Rachel was standing there. She gave Marissa a big smile.

"You're going to be great!" Rachel said. She hugged Marissa. Then she hurried out the door.

The dancers all headed backstage to hear Madame Stone's final instructions. As the locker room emptied out, Marissa continued sitting on her bench.

She hadn't even taken off her sneakers yet. She felt frozen. She couldn't go out there. She just couldn't.

Rachel's worried face appeared in the locker room door for a moment. Then it disappeared. Marissa still didn't move. She didn't touch the red leotard sitting next to her.

After a few minutes, Marissa heard someone else come in the locker room, but she didn't turn around. Then the person sat down on the bench next to her. Marissa finally looked up. It was Kelly.

Chapter 9

KELLY'S CONFESSION

Marissa scowled when she saw Kelly. "What are you doing here?" Marissa asked. She knew she was being rude, but she didn't care. Kelly was the last person she wanted to see.

Kelly seemed nervous. She looked down at her feet. Finally, she took a deep breath. "I wanted to tell you that I'm sorry for making fun of you," she said. "Clarice and I didn't mean it." Kelly blushed.

Marissa could hardly believe her ears. Kelly was apologizing!

"If you didn't mean it, why'd you do it?" Marissa asked.

She could hear the noise of the audience outside. She glanced up at the big wall clock. Ten minutes until the recital began.

Kelly shrugged. "I don't know," she said quietly.

"Well, you really made me feel bad," Marissa said.

Kelly nodded. "I know. I'm sorry. The recital's supposed to start in ten minutes. We all really, really want you to come out and dance. We can't do it without a Rose Fairy. Will you please come?" she asked.

Marissa glanced at the costume next to her. "I don't know," she whispered.

"You'll be really great," Kelly said. "The only reason Clarice and I were so mean is that we were totally jealous of you."

Marissa stared at Kelly. "You were jealous of me?" she repeated.

Kelly nodded. "Yeah. I know it was a really rotten thing to do. It's just that you're a way better dancer than any of us."

The audience was louder outside. It sounded like the place was packed. Marissa thought of her parents and grandparents sitting out there, holding their programs and cameras, all ready to see her perform. She glanced again at the red leotard.

"I want to dance," Marissa said quietly. "It's just this costume."

Kelly looked at the leotard. "What's wrong with it?" she asked.

"I can't put it on. I look so big in it. I feel like everyone's going to laugh at me," Marissa admitted. She couldn't believe she was actually telling Kelly how she felt. On the wall, the clock ticked. Five minutes until the recital was supposed to begin.

Kelly narrowed her eyes. She leaned forward until her face was almost touching Marissa's. "Listen to me," she said. "Don't worry about how you look. Just dance like you danced the day of the auditions. That's all that matters."

Outside, the audience got quiet. Marissa could hear Madame start to talk. She was giving her welcome speech to the parents before the curtain went up. There were two minutes left.

Marissa stood up. She grabbed the leotard and tutu.

"I'll be backstage in one minute," she said. Kelly's face lit up. She rushed out of the locker room.

Quickly, Marissa changed into the tights, leotard, and tutu. She hadn't worn real dance clothes in so long that the fabric felt weird against her skin. Her mind was whirling.

She wasn't sure she could do it. Could she dance like she'd danced on the day of the auditions?

Chapter 10

THE ROSE FAIRY

The rest of the dancers were standing in a little group backstage when Marissa ran in and joined them.

The curtain was still down. Madame was finishing her speech.

Marissa looked carefully at the girls to see if anyone was laughing at her in her leotard, but she saw only relief on their faces.

She didn't have time to think anymore, because outside the curtain, Andy was playing the opening music.

The dancers rushed to take their places. Marissa stood in the middle of the stage, both arms held gracefully out to the sides.

The curtain rose. Marissa was almost dazzled by the bright lights, but she didn't hear any laughter from the audience. They gasped with delight as she leapt across the stage.

Marissa felt stiff for the first few steps. But as she danced, she started really listening to Andy's playing. The music was so beautiful. Marissa felt like her body wanted to soar right above the audience.

Marissa stopped thinking and started just dancing. She moved with the music.

When the recital ended, she could hardly believe she was actually Marissa, instead of the Rose Fairy.

She held the final position, with all the dancers in a circle around her. The audience burst into applause. The clapping sounded like thunder. Marissa could hear people yelling, "Bravo! Bravo!" Her heart was pounding.

She had done it! She had danced like she was the Rose Fairy. No one had laughed. Instead, they were applauding!

The dancers lined up and joined hands the way Madame had taught them. They bowed to the audience as the curtain came down. Once the audience couldn't see them, all of the dancers started jumping up and down and hugging each other.

Rachel grabbed Marissa and gave her a big hug. "You did it!" she said. "I knew you would! That was amazing."

"You were amazing too," Marissa said, hugging her back.

"What happened?" Rachel said. "I thought you weren't going to put on the leotard."

"I wasn't," Marissa replied.

Just then, she caught Kelly's eye. Kelly gave her a little nod and a smile.

After a second, Marissa smiled back. "I had a little help at the end," she told Rachel. "But I think I had it in me the whole time. I just didn't know it."

ABOUT THE AUTHOR

Emma Carlson Berne has written more than a dozen books for children and young adults, including teen romance novels, biographies, and history books. She lives in Cincinnati, Ohio with her husband, Aaron, her son, Henry, and her dog, Holly.

ABOUT THE ILLUSTRATOR

When Tuesday Mourning was a little girl, she knew she wanted to be an artist when she grew up. Now, she is an illustrator who lives in South Pasadena, CA. She especially loves illustrating books for kids and teenagers. When she isn't illustrating, Tuesday loves spending time with her husband, who is an actor, and their two sons.

GLOSSARY

arabesque (air-uh-BESK)—to stand on one leg, with the other leg extended behind the body

audition (aw-DISH-uhn)—a tryout

ballerina (bal-uh-REE-nuh)—a female ballet dancer

barre (BAR)—a bar that helps dancers exercise

demonstrate (DEM-uhn-strate)—to show others how to do something

leotard (LEE-uh-tard)—a tight, one-piece garment worn for dancing

plie (plee-AY)—a movement in which a dancer bends her knees to the sides

recital (ree-SYE-tuhl)—a performance

self-conscious (self-KON-shuhss)—worried about what other people think

tutu (TOO-too)—a short ballet skirt made out of several layers of stiff net

More About Anna Pavlova

Anna Pavlova is widely considered to have been the most famous ballerina of all time. She was born on February 12, 1881, in St. Petersburg, Russia. She never knew her father, and her mother was a poor laundress.

When Anna was eight years old, her mother took her to a performance of the ballet *Sleeping Beauty*. Seeing that performance was the first thing that made Anna interested in ballet. She auditioned for a special ballet school, but she wasn't admitted because the people at the school thought she was too young and small.

Two years later, at the age of ten, Anna finally entered the Imperial Ballet School. Her first role was as a cupid in a ballet called *A Fairy Tale*.

At that time, ballerinas were expected to be small and compact, but Anna was not. She was thin, and she had long legs, thin ankles, and very high arches on her feet. She had to work hard to become accepted as a ballerina, since her physical appearance was different from what people expected.

Because she had trouble standing in the traditional ballerina shoes, Anna added a piece of wood to the toe of her ballet slippers. They would eventually become the modern pointe shoes, now worn by ballerinas everywhere.

Even though she didn't look like other dancers, Anna was soon the most famous ballerina in the world. She was most famous for her dance *The Dying Swan*. Anna died in 1931 at the age of 50.

DISCUSSION QUESTIONS

1. What are some ways to help a friend who is feeling badly?

2. Clarice and Kelly are mean to Marissa in this book because they are jealous of her. What are some reasons that people are jealous of others? What are some good ways to deal with jealousy?

3. Marissa feels like she is bigger than everyone else in her ballet class. She feels uncomfortable in her leotard. What could she have done to feel better about herself?

WRITING PROMPTS

1. Marissa feels self-conscious about her body. Write about a time when you felt self-conscious. What happened? How did you get over it?

2. In this book, Marissa's best friend encourages her to try out for the part of the Rose Fairy. Write about your best friend. Has your friend ever encouraged you?

3. Sometimes it's interesting to think about a story from another person's point of view. Try writing chapter 9 from Kelly's point of view. What does she see, hear, and say? How does she feel? How is the story different?